Introducti

The Llove Llama is a story of a quest for friendship taken by a brave and adorable llama named Llove, who takes a trip around the world searching for her new best friend – the Child Reader!

On each of the 7 continents, Llove meets a new friend who sends her North, South, East, and West on her fun-filled adventure around the world!

ISBN: 978-1-7362829-0-8

Library of Congress: 2020924451

BOOK ENDEAVORS

Dedications

To an always guiding light in my life,
Grammy Dot,
and my loving family,
Kevin, Karissa, and Ronnie
~ MTK ~

For my shining stars that light up my life –
Piper, Finnian, Greer, and Noirin
~ SC ~

The Llove Llama is the first of an 8-book series,

The Llove Llama & Friends.

Each friend that Llove meets on her world adventure
has its own story to tell.

The Llove Llama

travels the 7 continents to find friendship.

Ned the Narwhal

voyages the 5 oceans learning lessons along the way.

Bob the Sloth

finally gets moving and discovers the beauty of South America.

Donut the Dingo Dog

takes a walk around Australia and explores the Outback.

Charli the Cheetah

races through the vast land of Africa meeting new animals.

Ruby the Red Panda

discovers the unique wonders of Asia.

Peppermint the Penguin

teaches the world about Antarctica's environmental concerns.

Brave Feather the Owl

flies about Europe experiencing new cultures and people.

www.thellovellamaandfriends.com

The Llove Llama
Travels the 7 Continents

Written by

Monica Talbot-Kerkes & Sharla Charpentier

Illustrated by

Aljon Inertia

Arctic Ocean

Europe

Asia

Africa

Pacific
Ocean

Indian
Ocean

Australia

Antarctica

Once upon a time,
not so very long ago,
The Llove Llama was born
in a cozy bungalow.

The Llove Llama was fluffy white.
She had long eyelashes and big eyes.
Her ears were shaped like little hearts.
"PERFECT," her Mama and Papa sighed.

SOUTH AMERICA was a beautiful place
for The Llove Llama to grow up.
She played with llama friends all day
on the grassy mountaintops.

The Llove Llama had a dream
to find a special girl or boy.
She wanted a new FRIEND
to share LOVE, FUN, and JOY!

The Llove Llama was brave
and started on her way.
She entered the Amazon forest,
where it rained every day.

Hiiiii

The rainforest had yellow snakes,
blue frogs, and butterflies.
The Llove Llama was really lost.
Then a weird voice said, "Hiiiii."

The Llove Llama looked up.
WOW! It was a Sloth named Bob!
Leaves and twigs were in his hair.
Bob looked like quite a slob.

Chilling in a hammock,
munching on green leaves,
Bob wore socks with polka dots
pulled up to his knees.

"I need to find my friend!" LLove cried.
Bob said, "No prob-llama. Go SOUTH."
He pointed his long claw slowly,
then stuffed more leaves in his mouth.

The Llove Llama found a sturdy ship
and sailed South with the stars.
The next day she saw a bright white land.
Could it be the planet Mars?????

A purple flag said ANTARCTICA.
It was freeeeezing cold.
But the snow was oh so wonderful,
and the sun shone down like gold.

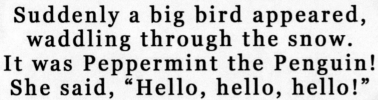

Suddenly a big bird appeared,
waddling through the snow.
It was Peppermint the Penguin!
She said, "Hello, hello, hello!"

Peppermint the Penguin
was lopsided, round, and fat.
She was black and white and pink
and wore a candy hat.

"Could you please help me?" Llove asked.
Peppermint nodded, "Why, yes."
Then they sipped their hot chocolate
and played a game of chess.

Peppermint sent The Llove Llama EAST on an ice cube.
After many lonely days, Llove yelled, "Land ahoy!"
It was the continent of AUSTRALIA.
OH BOY! OH BOY! OH BOY!

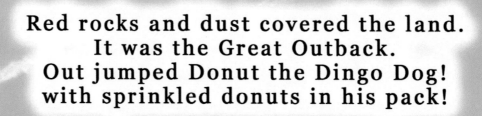

Red rocks and dust covered the land.
It was the Great Outback.
Out jumped Donut the Dingo Dog!
with sprinkled donuts in his pack!

"G'day Mate!" said Donut,
as The Llove Llama looked around.
"What's a llama like you doing
in this here part of town?"

"I'm looking for my friend," Llove said.
The dog scratched his scruffy ear.
He gave her a jelly donut
and replied, "Sorry, no children here."

They raced back to the great blue sea.
Donut patted The Llove Llama's head.
"If you run into trouble, good friend,
look for the narwhal. His name is Ned."

The Llove Llama swam out but tired.
Llove shouted, "PLEASE HELP ME!"
Up came Ned the Narwhal!
the naughty unicorn of the sea!

Ned shook his rainbow horn.
He demanded, "What is it you wish?
What are you doing, Girl,
out here with sharks and fish!?!"

The Llove Llama grabbed Ned's tail,
and he swam her to a beach.
"Welcome to AFRICA," Ned said.
Then he gave a little speech.

"Don't ever do this again.
Stay on your own turf!
Don't swim in MY ocean,
and don't ever try to surf!"

The Llove Llama roamed Africa,
through a land of grass and dust.
"I can't go on!" Llove cried.
Then a kind voice said, "You must."

It was Charli the Cheetah!
a lady cat with black heart spots.
Charli said, "My Dear, come to my tree."
I can see you're tired and hot."

The next day The Llove Llama saw zebras,
giraffes, hippos, and elephants too.
One elephant gave her a shower.
He even used shampoo!!!

Charli carried The Llove Llama to ASIA.
Bamboo grew near and far.
Then The Llove Llama saw Ruby the Red Panda!
with her paw in a candy jar!

Ruby looked more like a fox,
with white whiskers and a ringed tail.
"What do you need?" she asked
as she admired her sparkly nails.

"I need to find my friend," said Llove.
Ruby waved her lollipop WEST.
She gave The Llove Llama a red one.
"Take strawberry. It's the best."

The Llove Llama galloped to EUROPE
through many foreign places.
"Hola! Bonjour! Hallo! Ciao!"
called out people of many races.

One night under the magnificent moon,
she met a bird with splendid feathers.
It was Brave Feather the Owl!
who could scout the seas and weather!

Brave Feather flew The Llove Llama to NORTH AMERICA.
"Here is your home!" Brave Feather said.
The Llove Llama's heart filled with joy
when she found – YOU – her new best friend!!!

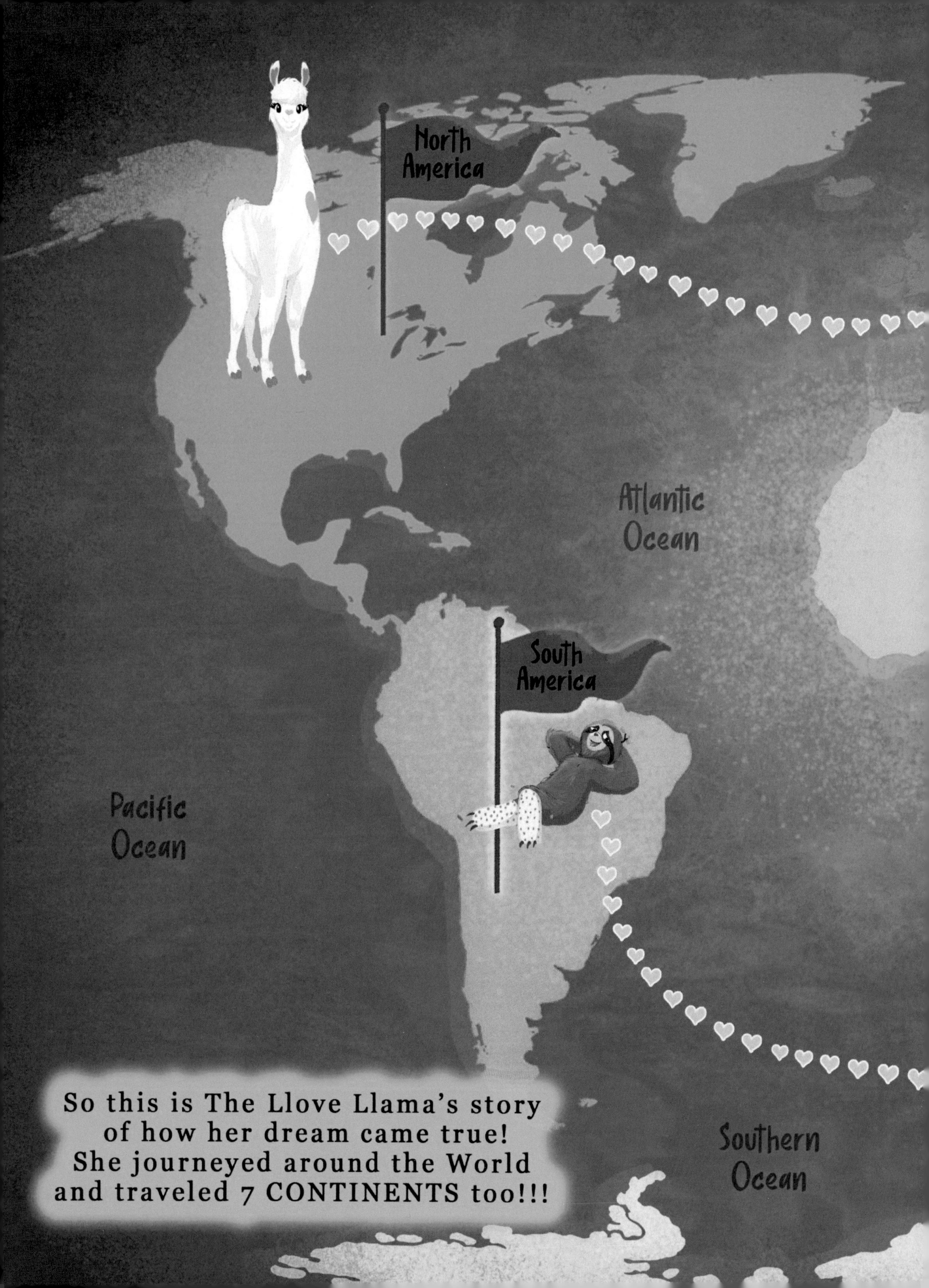

North America

South America

Atlantic Ocean

Pacific Ocean

Southern Ocean

So this is The Llove Llama's story of how her dream came true! She journeyed around the World and traveled 7 CONTINENTS too!!!

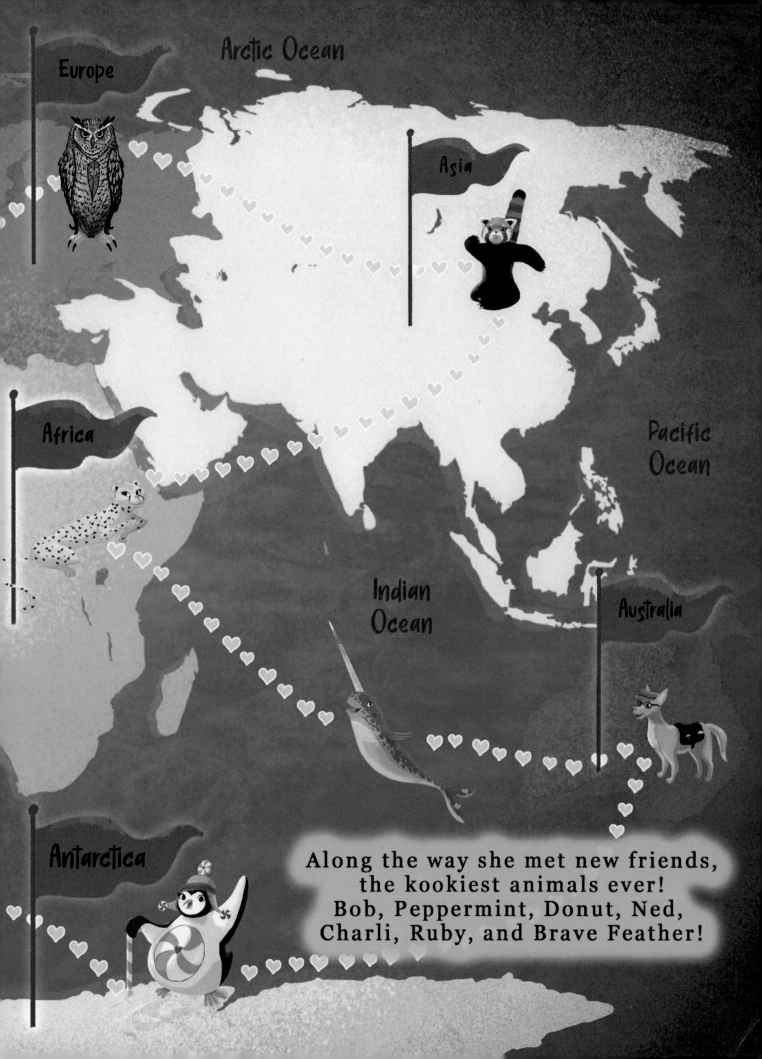

Arctic Ocean

Europe

Asia

Africa

Pacific Ocean

Indian Ocean

Australia

Antarctica

Along the way she met new friends,
the kookiest animals ever!
Bob, Peppermint, Donut, Ned,
Charli, Ruby, and Brave Feather!

You and The Llove Llama are now great FRIENDS,
and FRIENDSHIP is the BEST!!!
With friends you'll find your way in life,
no matter NORTH, SOUTH, EAST, or WEST!

Discussion Questions

1. Describe each animal character in the story and its personality. Which character is your favorite? Why?

2. What is the name of the continent where Llove is born? Describe the natural habitat where llamas live.

3. Why does Llove travel the seven continents? What difficulties does she encounter on her journey?

4. How does Llove show bravery? When have you shown bravery?

5. Describe the Amazon rainforest where Bob lives. Can you think of any other animals that live in the Amazon?

6. What compass direction does Bob send Llove? What are the four compass directions?

7. What continent does Peppermint live on? Can you think of any threats to this icy environment?

8. Which animal character helps Llove across an ocean? Do you like this character? Why or why not?

9. Llove's dream is to find her new best friend. Why is friendship important? How can you be a good friend?

10. Which continents would you like to travel? Why?

Llamas

Habitat: Llamas' natural habitat is the Andes Mountains in South America.

Facts

❖ Baby llamas are called 'crias'. Cria means creation.

❖ Llamas are 'herbivores', meaning they only eat plants.

❖ Llama poop doesn't stink!

Threats: Thankfully, they are not endangered as of yet.

Sloths

Habitat: Sloths live mostly in the tropical forests of Central & South America.

Facts

❖ Sloths sleep up to 20 hours a day and are the slowest mammal on the planet.

❖ Sloths go to the bathroom only once a week!

❖ Sloths spend about 90% of their lives hanging upside down in trees.

Threats: The Pygmy Three-toed Sloth (Dwarf) is one of the top 100 critically endangered animals due to habitat loss and destruction.

Penguins

Habitat: Most penguins live in and around Antarctica.

Facts

- ❖ Penguins are flightless birds. They have adapted flippers to swim in water.

- ❖ The male Emperor Penguin incubates the eggs for about 2 months, not the females!

- ❖ Penguins live in large groups to protect themselves from predators like sharks.

Threats: About 2/3 of penguin species are threatened due largely to global warming, making them one of the most endangered seabirds.

Dingo Dogs

Habitat: Dingo dogs (dingoes) are found primarily in Australia.

Facts

- ❖ Dingoes are the largest land predators in Australia.

- ❖ Dingoes are 'carnivores', which means they eat meat.

- ❖ Dingoes rarely bark. Instead, they howl like wolves.

Threats: Most dingoes are 'hybrids', meaning they are part pure dingo and part dog. The pure dingo is very near extinction.

Narwhals

Habitat: Narwhals are found in the Arctic Ocean.

Facts

- ❖ People often refer to a narwhal as the "unicorn of the sea" because of its long horn.

- ❖ The horn is actually a tooth that can grow up to 9 feet long!

- ❖ Narwhals live up to 50 years. They change color as they age.

Threats: Narwhals are not endangered as of yet. However, they have been identified as 'special concern', meaning they could easily become endangered.

Cheetahs

Habitat: Almost all cheetahs live in the plains and bushy areas in Africa.

Facts

- ❖ Cheetahs are the fastest land mammals on our planet!

- ❖ Cheetahs are part of the 'big cat' family along with lions, tigers, cougars, and leopards.

- ❖ Cheetahs have black tear lines to keep the sun out of their eyes.

Threats: Cheetahs are the most endangered of all the big cats due to loss of habitat and prey.

Red Pandas

Habitat: Red pandas are located mostly in the Himalaya Mountains in Asia.

Facts

- ❖ Red pandas spend about 90% of their time in trees and eat bamboo.

- ❖ Red pandas use their ringed tails as pillows!

- ❖ Red pandas are known as 'forest acrobats.' They use their tails to balance themselves in the trees.

Threats: There are less than 10,000 red pandas left in the world due to habitat loss, poachers who hunt them for their fur, and illegal pet trade.

Owls

Habitat: Owls live in all parts of the world except Antarctica.

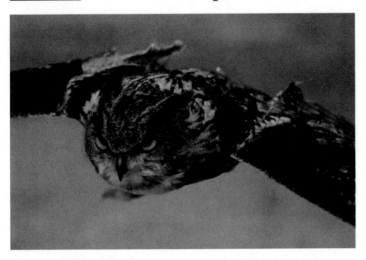

Facts

- ❖ There are around 250 different species of owls.

- ❖ Owls are 'nocturnal', meaning they are active at night.

- ❖ Owls are silent fliers. Shhh!

Threats: The Barn Owl and the Northern Spotted Owl are endangered. Other owl species are at risk due to habitat loss, climate change, and pesticide use.

Coming Soon

NED THE NARWHAL
VOYAGES THE 5 OCEANS

**THE LLOVE LLAMA HAS FOUND YOU!
BUT THIS STORY ISN'T THE END.
NOW TRAVEL ALL 5 OCEANS
ON AN ADVENTURE WITH NARWHAL NED!!!**

About the Authors

Monica Talbot–Kerkes & Sharla Charpentier

Monica and Sharla are cousins and soul sisters who share a passion for writing creative children's stories, a love for teaching, family, travel, adventure, and all of the world's amazing creatures – most certainly llamas!

Monica is a mother of two, an English as a Second Language teacher, writer, and poet. She created the original storyline for *The Llove Llama* and found her imagination and love of rhyme to shine best in children's books.

Sharla is a mother of four, a lawyer, artist, writer, and poet. She created *The Llove Llama* character, co-authored *The Llove Llama*, and brought to life *The Llove Llama and Friends* characters through her character drawings.

Monica and Sharla are making their dreams of writing adventurous and educational children's books come true. Their vision is to inspire, teach, and positively impact children while bringing awareness to world crises.

Visit: www.thellovellamaandfriends.com
Follow Monica and Sharla on Instagram @thellovellama

About the Illustrator

Aljon Inertia

Aljon specializes in creating beautiful, one-of-a-kind illustrations for children's books. His goal and purpose in life are to bring his passion for illustration to children's books that speak to good morals and values while providing lessons to today's youth.

Aljon's colorful illustrations bring engagement to the author's content, so the story comes alive on the book's pages. His creative illustrations are published in children's books worldwide.

Follow Aljon on Instagram @inertiaillustrator

Made in the USA
Middletown, DE
23 December 2020